Fairytale Frankie

and the Tricky Witch

For Anne – G G ★ For my wonderful teacher Mrs Wood who inspired so many x – SL

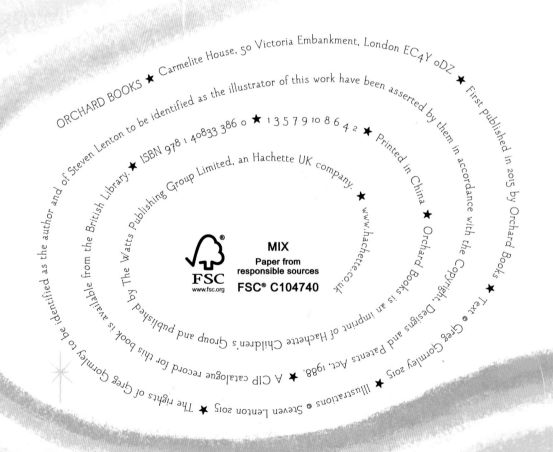

ORCHARD BOOKS ★ Carmelite House, 50 Victoria Embankment, London EC4Y 0DZ ★ First published in 2015 by Orchard Books ★ Text © Greg Gormley 2015 ★ Illustrations © Steven Lenton 2015 ★ The rights of Greg Gormley to be identified as the author and of Steven Lenton to be identified as the illustrator of this work have been asserted by them in accordance with the Copyright, Designs and Patents Act, 1988. ★ A CIP catalogue record for this book is available from the British Library. ★ ISBN 978 1 40833 386 0 ★ 1 3 5 7 9 10 8 6 4 2 ★ Printed in China ★ Orchard Books is an imprint of Hachette Children's Group and published by The Watts Publishing Group Limited, an Hachette UK company. ★ www.hachette.co.uk

MIX
Paper from
responsible sources
FSC® C104740
FSC
www.fsc.org

Fairytale Frankie

and the Tricky Witch

Greg Gormley

Steven Lenton

ORCHARD

Frankie **loved** fairytales.
She **really**, **really** loved them.
So, one morning, she was rather
surprised and delighted to find . . .

. . . a **fairytale** **princess** in her bedroom!

"Please could you help me to hide?" said the princess. "THE WITCH IS COMING!"

"Yes, of course!" said Frankie. "You can hide under my bed."

Then Frankie opened her bedroom door only to find
a **unicorn's bottom** blocking her path.

"I don't know where to hide," said the unicorn, panicking,
"AND THE WITCH IS ON HER WAY!"

This was all quite unusual but Frankie adored unicorns,
so she pushed it into her wardrobe.

"Please could you pass my dungarees?" she asked,
before carefully closing the door.

Frankie got dressed and went to the bathroom, where she noticed a **mermaid** peeping out from the bath. "WOW! Hello!" said Frankie.

"Shhhhhhh," whispered the mermaid,
"I'm **hiding** from the **witch**. Would you help me?"
"Of course!" said Frankie, as she drew the
shower curtain. "That should do the trick."

Frankie zipped downstairs.
"If the witch **is** coming, I ought
to find my sensible shoes, just in
case I need to run," said Frankie.

She heard a
clinKing
sound and saw
two boots
sticking out from
under the coats . . . .

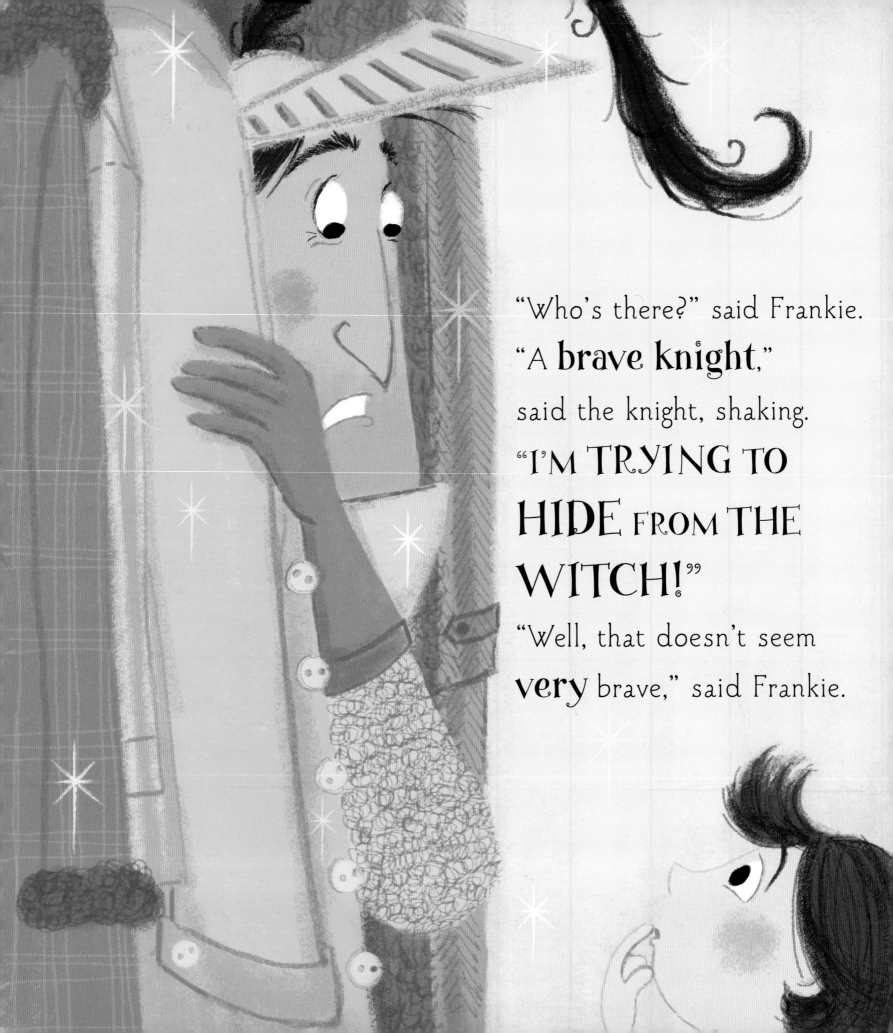

"Who's there?" said Frankie.
"A **brave knight**,"
said the knight, shaking.
"**I'M TRYING TO HIDE FROM THE WITCH!**"
"Well, that doesn't seem **very** brave," said Frankie.

"You'd better come and have some breakfast."
Frankie gave the knight a piece of toast then hid
him amongst the pots and pans under the sink.

As Frankie poured her cereal, a small **frog** hopped out of the box – cruNch!

"What are you doing in my breakfast?" said Frankie.

"Hiding," said the frog.

"Well, jump back in the box then," said Frankie.

"Can I have a kiss?" asked the frog.

"Certainly not," said Frankie as the doorbell rang.

There was a **king** at the door.
"Don't tell me," said Frankie, "you need to hide from the witch."
"Correct," said the king. "Somewhere posh and fit for royalty, please!"

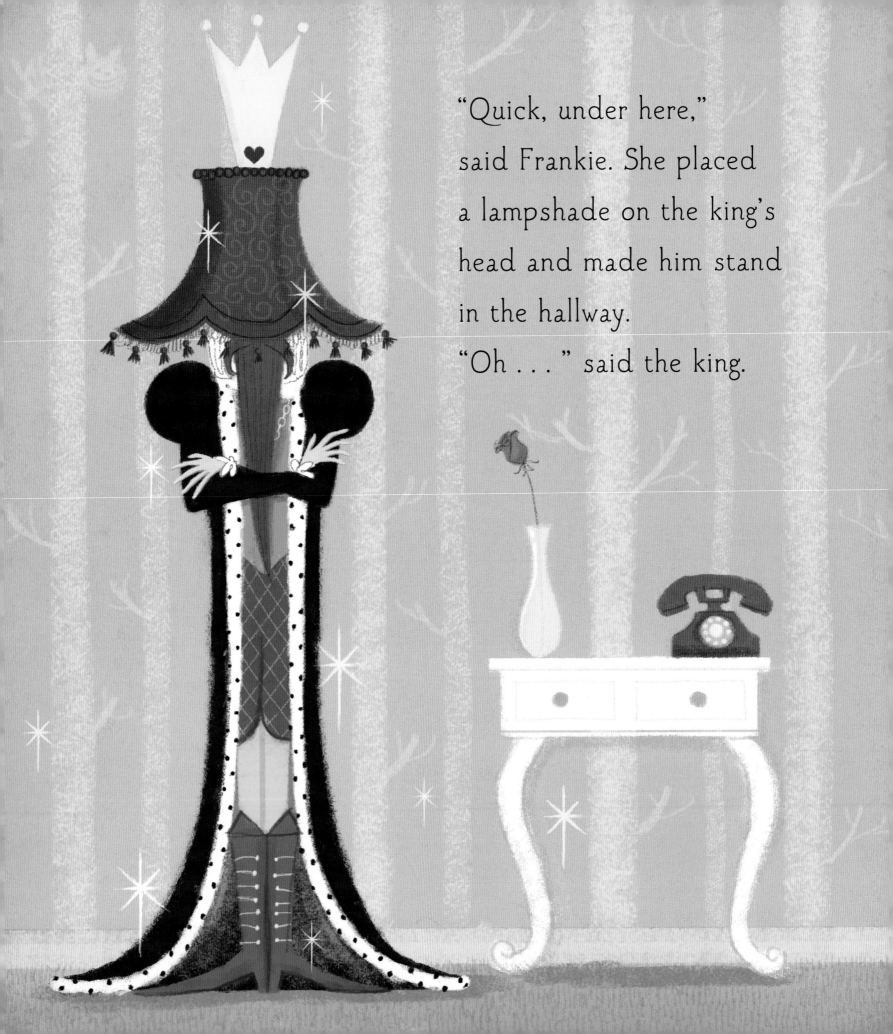

"Quick, under here,"
said Frankie. She placed
a lampshade on the king's
head and made him stand
in the hallway.

"Oh . . . " said the king.

Frankie looked around.
She had hidden everyone.
"But who will hide me?"
said Frankie.
It was too late...

KA ZHAM!

The door crashed open and THE WITCH appeared in a puff of smoke. "GOT YOU!" the witch shrieked. "Now, where are the others?"

Frankie wanted to run.
It took every bit of her courage
to say, "I don't know who you
could possibly mean."
"Then there's only one thing
for it!" said the witch, waving
her pointy fingers in the air.
"BROOM, BROOM,
BRING THEM TO ME!"

With a wh**OO**sh the witch's broomstick sped through the house. It swept the princess from under the bed. "Careful!" she said.

It shoved the unicorn out of the wardrobe. "How rude!" he said.

It brushed the mermaid out of the bath. "That tickles!" she laughed.

The broom waggled around under the sink until out clattered the knight – **clank!**

It tipped over the cereal and out tumbled the frog – **crackle!**

Finally, it knocked the lampshade off the king's head – **clonk!**

"Stop!" said Frankie. "LEAVE MY FRIENDS ALONE." But the witch just cackled, "I've found you ALL . . .

. . . whose **turn** is
it **now?**"

"Turn? What **do** you mean?"
asked Frankie, puzzled.
"We're playing **hide-and-seek,**"
said the king. "Would you
like to play too?"
"Oh, yes please!" said Frankie.
"I love hide-and-seek!"

"Smashing," said the witch. "Now shut your eyes and count to ten while we hide." Frankie shut her eyes and counted to ten, then she called . . .

"COMING, READY OR NOT!"